MW01026504

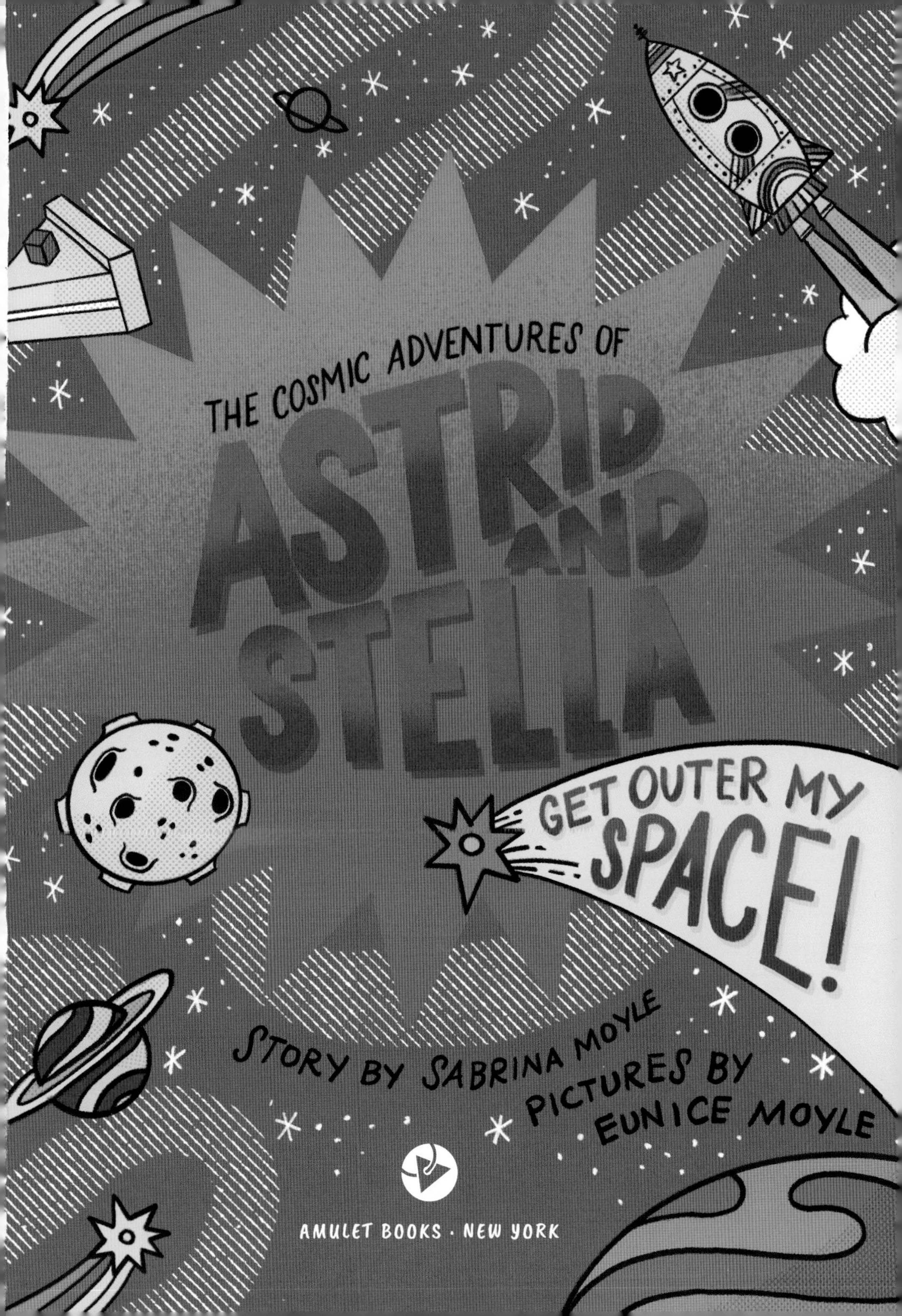
THE COSMIC ADVENTURES OF
ASTRID AND STELLA
GET OUTER MY SPACE!
STORY BY SABRINA MOYLE
PICTURES BY EUNICE MOYLE
AMULET BOOKS · NEW YORK

11
0

NO-O-METER

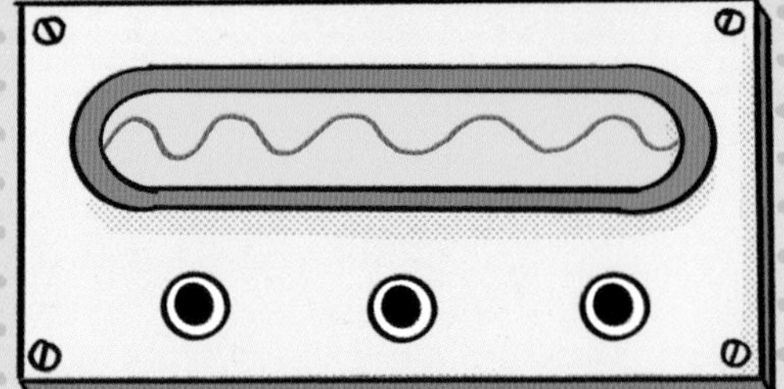

FEELINGS SENSOR
HAPPY

WE
COME
IN
PEACE

CONTENTS

LAUNCHPAD
LAUNCHPAD

CHAPTER ONE

GAME ON!

Gah!
I'm losing!
HA!!
Take THAT!
HIYAAA!
YAAAASSS!!!
Hey! STOP!
GAME OVER!! I WIN!!!
LAUNCHPAD

Whoop!
Whoop! Whoop!
I am the CHAMPION! I am the CAT'S MEOW!

NUTTIN' can stop me now! YOW!
BOOWAAHAHG

Astrid, I see you are feeling . . . UPSET.
UPSET
SAD/TIRED
CALM
HAPPY
EXCITED
FRUSTRATED
ANGRY

Stella . . .
wasn't . . .
playing FAIR!!!
WAAAAA!

Players do not always follow protocol.

Diaper for your face?

I CAN'T GET ONLINE!!!

No online games.
No cat videos.
No galaxy maps.

THAT'S IMPOSSIBLE! WE CAN'T LIVE WITHOUT CAT VIDEOS!!!

CHARADES,
anyone?

No galaxy
maps?!

How will we
go on adventures?!

We're . . .
we're . . .

LOST
IN SPACE!!!!!

This is not amusing.

Input incoming.

BUREAU OF INTERSTELLAR AFFAIRS
Dear Everyone in the Universe,
We regret to inform you that Intergalactic Wi-Fi will be down for the next 8 hours. We apologize for the inconvenience.
Sincerely,
The Management

EIGHT HOURS?! That's FOREVER!!!!

This is an OUTRAGE!!!

OUR MISSION IS IN PERIL!!! WHAT WILL WE DO?!!!

Settle your tea kettle. We'll land until the "outrage" is over.

Where?!

There!

BARGLE
DORF
POP. 3,423,534-ISH, LAST TIME WE CHECKED!
JOIN NOW

Adventure calls.
INCOMING CALL: ADVENTURE

Initiate landing gear!
Touchdown!
BACK UP WIFI BOOSTER!
MEGAFUN GAMING LOUNGE
Where is everybody?
Um . . . having MEGA FUN!?!

So . . . what are
we waiting for?!
LET'S GO!!!

FART DEFENSE!
IT'S A GAS!
SPATULA SMACK DOWN!
IT'LL MAKE YOU FLIP!
TICKETS
Welcome! Three players?
Right this way.

SNAX
Cool!
Yum, yum, and MORE yum!
SNAX!
STAR CHIPS
FRIES
MORE FRIE
SHAKES
SOMETHING HEALTHY

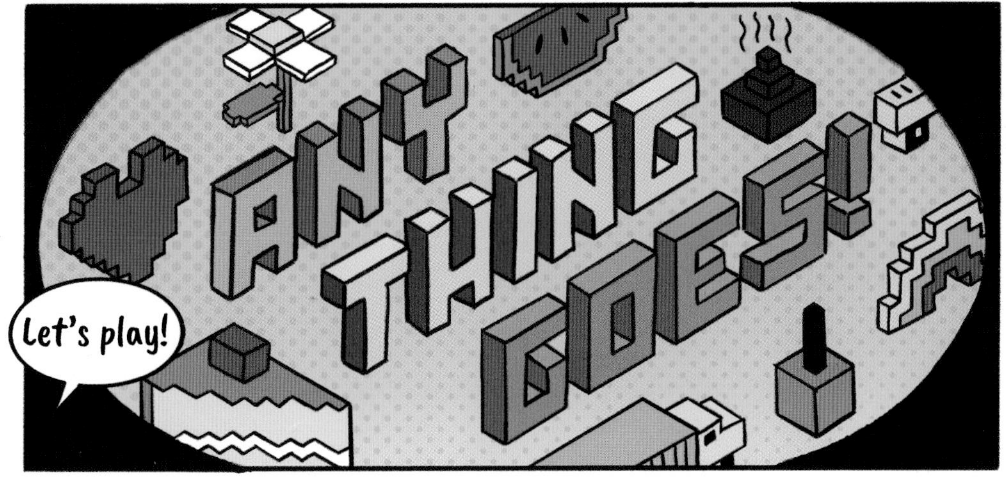
ANYTHING GOES!
Let's play!

Hee hee! Look at us!

This is AWESOME! What should we build?
How about . . .

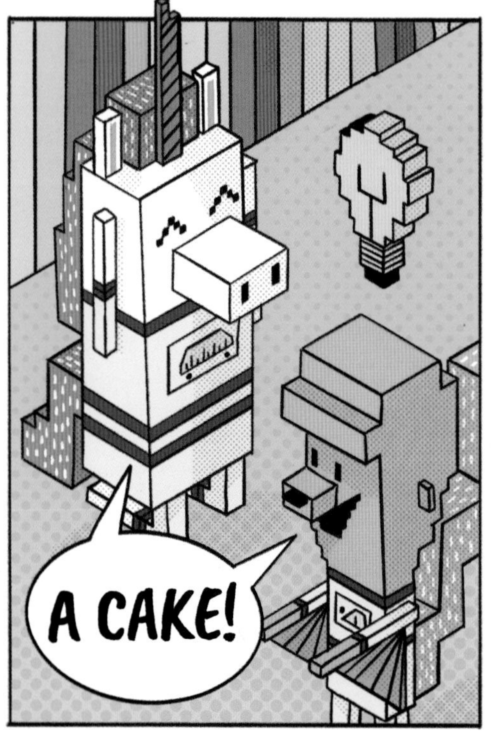
A CAKE!

It'll be hard, but I'm willing to WHISK it.

Let's BAKE this happen!

Together, we can BAKE the world a BATTER place.

VOILA! PERFECTION!

Yum!
I'll take that!
Hey!

You can't
do that!!!
NOM
NOM
NOM

AGH!!
DRAGON
BREATH!

This
game is WHISK-Y
business.

Poop chips? That's disgusting!
YUCK!
Hey, my MOM could build a better cake than you!
Yeah!
You call that a cake? More like a FAKE! Heh heh heh!

READY, AIM, FIRE!
BRUSSELS SPROUTS?!!!

GRRRR!!!

I'll show you . . .

TAKE THAT!

YAARR! ME EYE!!!!
BOINK!

I QUIT!!!!

That was a CAKE-TASTROPHE!

It's all FONDANT games until someone loses an eye . . .

. . . and then it all ends in TIERS.

Wait a second—LOOK!

We're not the only ones who are PIPING MAD!
SOAP

This is awful! Someone's going to get hurt!
Bobo, we've got to DO something!!
At your service.

ATTENTION, CARBON-BASED LIFE-FORMS!

!
?
?
!!
!?

We come in the Friend Ship, er, I mean, IN FRIENDSHIP!

Our analysis shows that you are feeling . . .
MEGA-MAD
ANGRY
UPSET
SAD/TIRED
CALM
HAPPY
EXCITED
FRUSTRATED

MEGA-MAD

YEAH!
ARRRR!

And that you may need . . .
NEEDS-O-NATOR

Respect?
NEEDS-O-NATOR
FRIENDSHIP RESPECT COURTESY KINDNESS COOPERAT

Yes! And kindness! Fairness! Cooperation!
Aye aye!

Analyzing . . .

May I recommend a Player Protocol?

He means "a set of rules" . . . !

Yeah!
Don't yuck my yum!
No poop throwing!
No stealing!
Don't meh my wow!

Excellent.

Output incoming . . .
-No Poop Throwing
-No Name Calling
-Be Respect-ful
Be Kind
-Don't Yuck My Yum
-Don't Meh My Wow
-Ask Permission
-Stay Positive
-Have Fun!

But . . . W-W-WAIT A SECOND! W-w-we can't just make up our own rules! W-w-what about . . . YOU-KNOW-WHO?!!!
GASP!

YEAH!!! If he finds out, we'll be in MEGA TROUBLE!!!

Who's You-Know-Who?

The Grand Pooh-bah.

He's . . . T-T-T-TERRIFYING!

His real name is . . .
WHISPHER
WHISPER

HA! You-Know-Who hasn't met our cosmic DREAM TEAM!

We've got this!

Fear doesn't scare us!

NEXT STOP: MEGAFUN HQ
We're going to see this Grand Pooh-bah Muckety-Muck You-Know-What!

TRAM-endous.
We'll fix this playtime pickle!

WELCOME
TO
MEGA
FUN
OPEN
24/7

WELCOM
PUG LIFE
We want to see the boss, the top dog . . .
The big cheese.

WELCOME
Follow the sign.
PUG LIFE
THE BIG CHEESE
Just another cheesy pun.

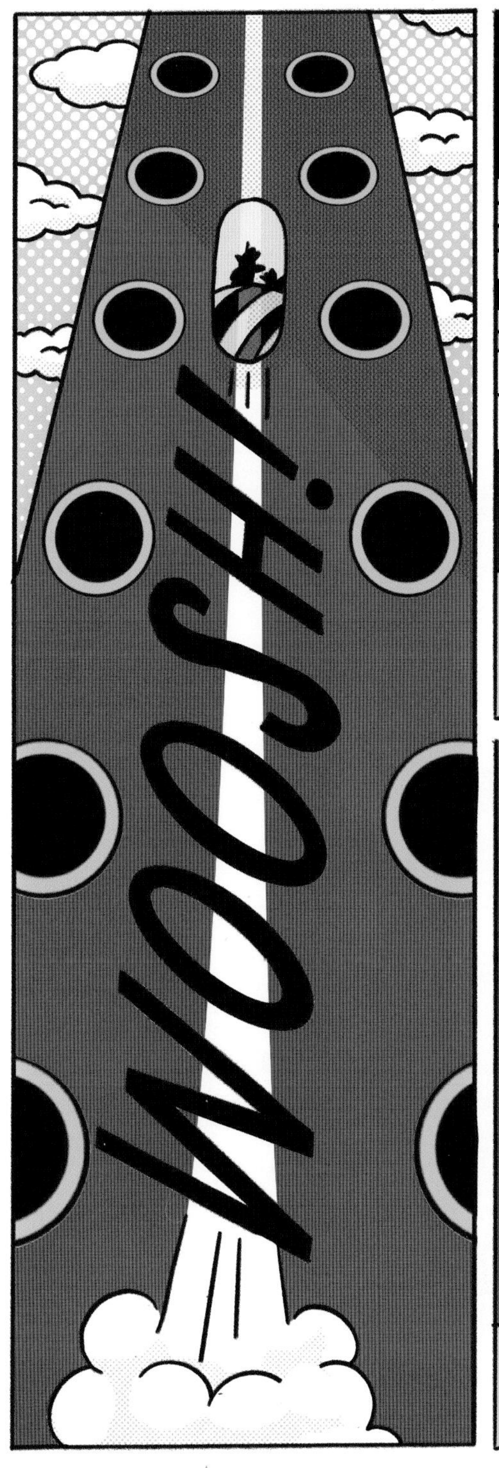
WOOSH!

DING!
Ahem. Excuse me.

Yes?

We're Astrid and Stella.

And I am . . .
EVIL SCREENIUS™!
MWAHAHA HAHA!
How can I help?

We have a MEGA problem.

Your games have NO RULES!

But we have a solution!

What is this?!

A Player Protocol to make your games FAIR and FUN!

NUMBER OF PLAYE
Silly squirrel!
My games are not designed to have FUN!

They are designed for me to DOMINATE!

How do I do it? I'll tell you my little secret . . .
I keep players FIGHTING . . .

24 HOUR BACKUP BOOSTER
...ALL DAY and ALL NIGHT thanks to my feeble furry friends! MWAHAHAHA!
GASP!
Hamsters under mind control! They're on a roll ... but not by choice!

That's terrible!

Isn't it, though?

But it APPEARS we don't SEE EYE TO EYE . . .
So I will need to . . .
HAMSTER-IZER!
HYPNOSIS MACHINE
ZzzzAPP!!
AAAARGH!!!

YOUR MINDS ARE MINE! MWAHAHAHA!!!!

EYE, EYE, sir!

I SEE what you're saying.

You are our BEST FRIEND . . .

System alert! Processing . . .

Synchronizing Slime Ray.
SLIME RAY

SCREEN TIME is over, Evil Screenius™!
HAMSTER-IZER!
HYPNOSIS MACHINE
SLIME RAY
NOOOoo

It's HAMSTERTIME!
Let's roll!

We demand a Player Protocol!

We'll never stop fighting for friendship!

NEITHER WILL WE!
Son of a hamster! I am outnumbered!

Our Player Protocol will help you attract players AND save friendship! And there's something else . . .
PLAYER PROTOCOL

Presenting the HAMSTAR SYSTEM.
HAMSTAR SYSTEM

Instead of collecting players . . .

. . . and cutie-patootie little oogie-woogie hamsters . . .

. . . you can collect HAMSTARS!
HAMSTAR SYSTEM
5
4.5
5
5
Five stars means players are having MEGA FUN, for reals!

I guess I could give it a whirl . . .

Well, would you look at the time!
It's been eight hours!

That means the Friend Ship is back online! HOORAY!

SLIME flies when you're having fun.
SLIME RAY

Time for us to . . .

Blast off!
Farewell, friends!

ZZZZ

CHAPTER TWO

DARE TO DREAM!

Astrid, are you awake?
No.

I can't sleep.
ZZZZ

Hey Astrid.
ZZZZZZ

Astrid.
ASTRID!!!

What?! What happened?! Are we there yet?!

I can't sleep.
Grrrr . . . You woke me up!!!

I'm having nightmares.
What kind of nightmares?
I . . . I can't say . . . It's . . . it's . . .

. . . TOO SCARY!!!
WAAA!!

Stella, it's OK. It might help to talk about it.

Is it monsters?
No . . .

Spiders?
No . . .

Zombies?

No . . . it's . . . it's . . .
SCARY BUNNIES!!!
Oh. Oh no. No no no NO NO!

That makes me think of . . .
EVIL CLOWNS!!!
BOBO!!!
YAWN. At your service.
WE CAN'T SLEEP!!!
WE'RE SCARED!!!

One moment . . .
COM
ZZZ CART

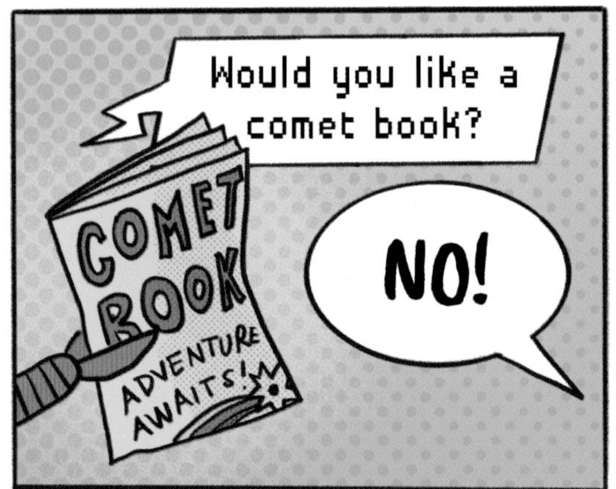
Would you like a comet book?
COMET BOOK
ADVENTURE AWAITS!
NO!

Glass of water?
NO!

Eye mask?
NO!

Night-light?
NO!

Whale song?
EEEEOOOOO
EEEEOOOO
EEEEOOO
NO!
Lavender mist?
Ack!
COUGH
NO.
Can you think happy thoughts?
NO!

This is my own worst nightmare.

WAAAAA!

I need my beauty rest.

Bobo, don't leave us!!!!

This is the 35th REM cycle interruption *this* week.
SLEEPYTIME
SLEEP TRACKER
M T W TH F
A
S
B

This could endanger our entire mission.

We're too scared to sleep, and even worse—

Too scared to DREAM!

How will we ever dream up NEW ADVENTURES!?

WHAT ARE WE GONNA DO??!!!

We must go to Wink 40 to find answers.
VISIT BEAUTIFUL WINK 40

Wink 40?
The planet of dreams.

How do you know it will help?

I've HERD good things.

I guess it's worth a try.

Fire up the turbo pumps.

BLAST OFF.

So many sheep!
This is BAAAA-nanas!
Hee hee!
BAAA 421
BAAA 36
BAAA 99
BAAA 88
BAAAA 4
BAAAAA 14,598
BAAA 3
BAAAA 108
BAAAA 33
BAAAA 15
BAAAAA 212
BAAAAA 1
BAAAA 8
BAAAAA 2,628
AAAA 65
BAAAA 11
BAAAA 46
BAAAAA 658
BAAAAA 9,583
BAAAAA 797

Welcome, friends.
Do you seek guidance?

Yes, we
can't sleep!
Our nightmares
are terrifying!
I see. Come
fly with me.

Whee!

Dreamy!

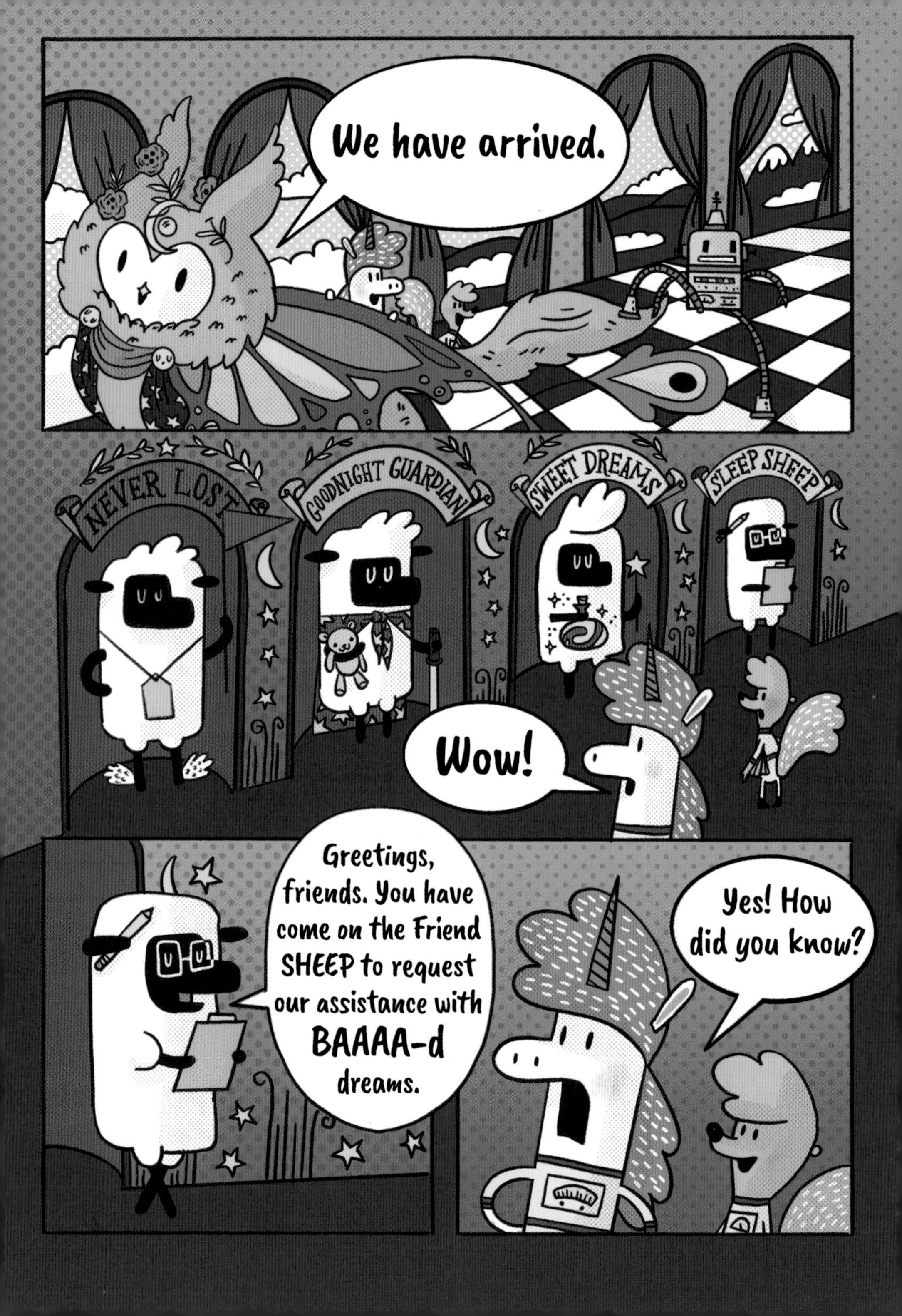
We have arrived.
NEVER LOST
GOODNIGHT GUARDIAN
SWEET DREAMS
SLEEP SHEEP
Wow!
Greetings, friends. You have come on the Friend SHEEP to request our assistance with BAAAA-d dreams.
Yes! How did you know?

We're experts in our FIELD.

Tell us, what BAAAA-thers you?

LIONS
WOLVES
SHARKS
SPIDERS
SNAKES
BUGS
SPINACH
GETTING LOST
WASHING HAIR
MONSTERS
FARTS
WEDGIES
CLOWNS
OTHER:

Clowns!
Evil bunnies!

I see. The Council will advise you.

Greetings. I am Never Lost. The world of dreams is big and scary. It can be easy to lose your way.

I offer you a GPS—Guaranteed Peaceful Sleep Tracker. With it, you will always find your way out of baaaa-d dreams.

Winged Roller Skates. These will help you quickly escape scary visions.

The Freedom Flag. When you are lost, you can follow it home.

I accept your gifts with a grateful heart.

I am Goodnight Guardian. Dreams can conjure up scary things. I give you these tools to defeat them.

The Blanket of Invisibility. Wear it and you can sneak past your enemies unseen.

The Night Saber. It will help you fricassee your foes.

The Bear-ier. It creates an unbreakable force field around you.

WOWEEE! THANKS!!!

I am Sweet Dreams. I make dreams delightful.

I offer you my Poof Potion. Drink it to make unwanted dreams go *POOF!*

Dream Dust. Sprinkle it to inspire beautiful dreams.

For you, my dear Bobo, Extreme Ear Plugs, to protect your beauty rest.
EXTREME EAR PLUGS

Much obliged.
EXTREME EAR PLUGS

You have your tools. Now, we wish you a b-EWE-tiful night's SHEEP!

How will we ever repay you?

Our tools are given freely to all those who ask.
STELLAR!

But you must believe in them for their powers to work.
And for that, we present you with a challenge: THE SLUMBER GAMES.
In these games, you will face your nightmares. Use the tools to find your way home.

GULP.
Gluck.

Don't worry, we will be watching over you.

SLUMBER GAMES
We can d-d-d-o hard things.

Quick!
The Blanket of
Invisibility!

Phew!
That was no SMALL FEET.

Say "Hello!" to my Night Saber!!!

BOING!
Bear-ier, ACTIVATE!!!
WOOSH!

Clear your plate!
Eat your veggies!
One more bite!
NOOOOOOOOO!!!!
Quick! The skates!

We did it!
The tools worked!
Woot.
Well done, dreamers. You passed the test.

Farewell, friends. It's PASTURE bedtime.

Thank EWE.

Back to the Friend SHEEP!

BAAAA-last off!

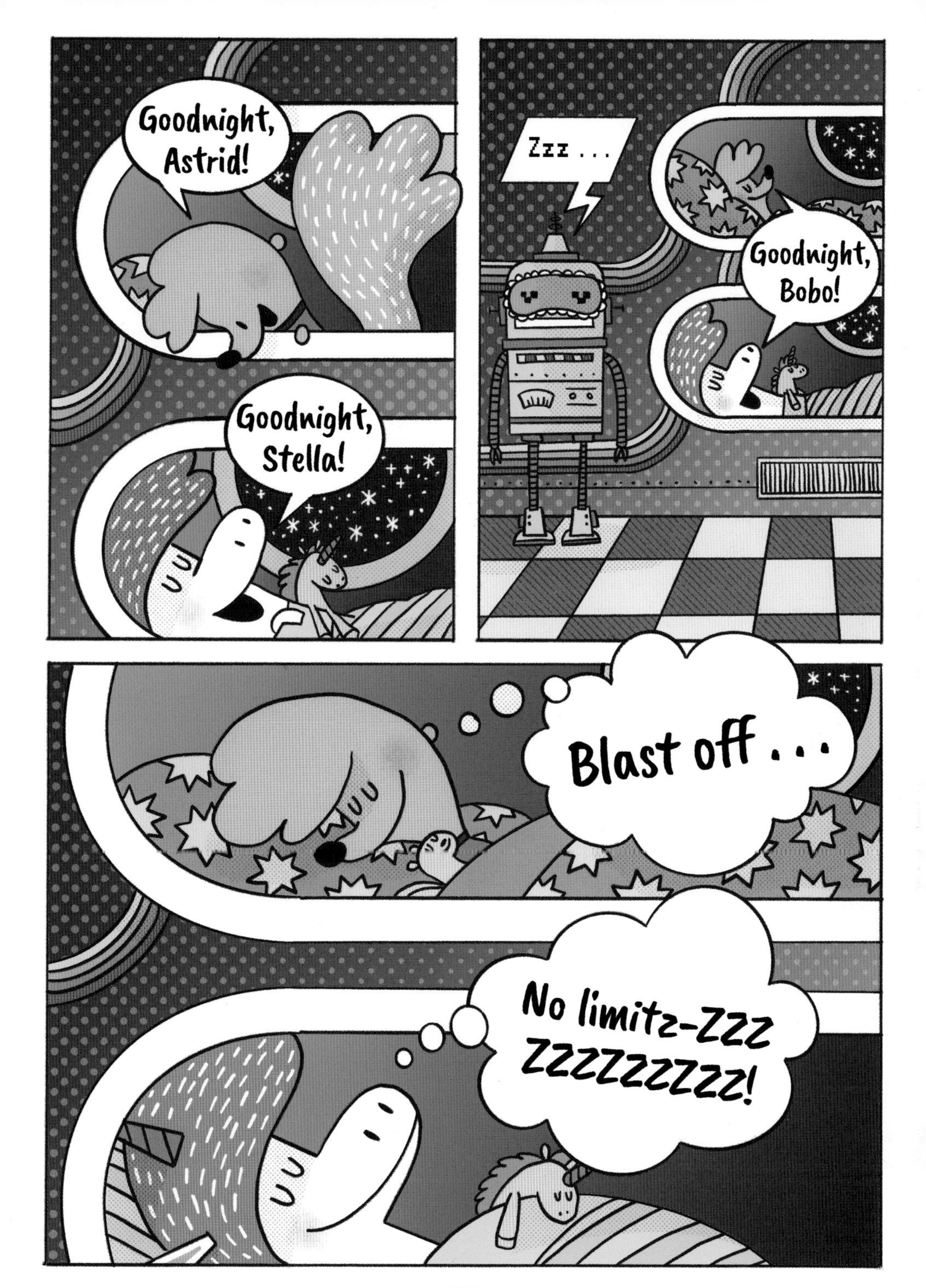
Goodnight, Astrid!
Goodnight, Stella!
Zzz . . .
Goodnight, Bobo!
Blast off . . .
No limitz-ZZZ ZZZZZZZZZ!

CHAPTER THREE

GET OUTER MY SPACE!

Hey, Bobo! Watcha doing?
Recharging my batteries.
SILENT FART
SPF 1000
SUN POWER
SOLAR
CHARGE
I could use some sun, too. We've been in space for light-years!
SILENT FART
Sigh! This is the good life!
SPF 1000

Hey guys!
Can I join you?
COMET BOOK
SILENT FART

There's no room . . .
COMET BOOK
SILENT FART

Sure there is!
I can fit right . . .

!!
HERE!
BOING!

Well, this is inconvenient . . .
ASTRID!
Oops.

THE NEXT DAY . . .
Hey, Bobo! Watcha doing?

I am making prototype FRIEND PODS.

To keep people OUTER MY SPACE.

I don't get it.

Friendship is the delicate art of connecting AND staying in your OWN space.
PERSONAL ZONE
1 ARM
50
T=G²/V
x=/y
FIG 2.
As you can see, all beings have an invisible personal space zone.
=1 ARM-O-METER
My Friend Pods will keep you "in the zone."
127
50
FRIENDSHIP POD

Getting outer your own space can be disastrous.
X-RAY : CAT
BURP!

Has that ever happened to **YOU?!**
GASP!

Yes. I have invaded others' space . . .

Like the time I lost my cool and caught my friend's head on fire.
BOBO ANGRY!!!!
Eep!

And others have invaded my space . . .

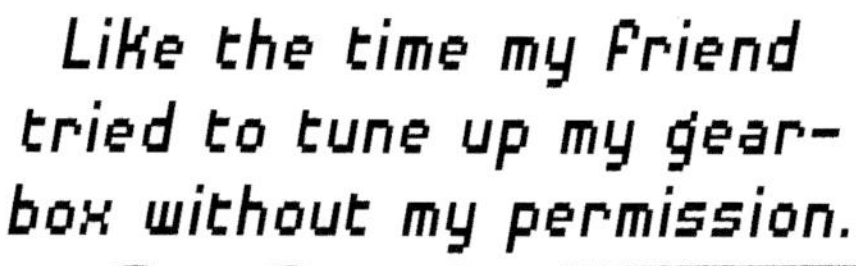

Like the time my friend tried to tune up my gear-box without my permission.

INTRUDER ALERT!
I was just trying to help!

Oh. Have I invaded people's space, too?

I calculate the odds at . . . 100%.
BEEP!
BOOP!

Huh. Like the time I told Stella she wasn't magical because she's just a squirrel?

Apparently so.

I'm sorry, Stella.
I forgive you.
SNIFF!

The Friend Pods will solve these problems by creating a clear boundary . . .

NO-O-METER
NOPE
NO WAY
FEELINGS SENSOR
HAPPY
ALL
CLEAR
RESPECT-O-METER
YOU DO YOU
MY WAY OR THE HIGHWAY
SPONSE METER
CURIOSITY
LISTENING
ON
OFF
EMPATHIZER
TRANSLATO
INPUT
...and equipping you with your own personal space controls.
POWER CORE

Cool!
Can I try?
We'll need space to test them . . .
Perfect!
UNINHABITED MOON POPULATION:0
Fire up the turbo pumps!
BLAST OFF!

WHEEEEEEEE!!!

This is AWESOME!
Look at ME!

Watch me spin! This is SO MUCH FUN! You wanna try?!
NO WAY! Spinning makes me wanna BARF!
NO-O-METER
NOPE
NOWAY
FEELINGS SENSOR
BARF
CLEAR
RESPECT-O-METER
YOU DO YOU
MY WAY OR THE HIGHWAY
CURIOSITY
LISTENING
ON
OFF
EMPATHIZER

This looks cool! Astrid, come see!

Nah, I'll wait here while you explore!
FEELINGS SENSOR
SCARED
RESPECT-O-METER
YOU DO YOU
MY WAY OR THE HIGHWAY
TRANSLATOR
INPUT

Aw, c'mon. Stop being such a scaredy-corn! You NEVER want to have any fun!

GRRR . . . !!!
FEELINGS SENSOR
ANGRY
RESPECT-O-METER
MY WAY OR THE HIGHWAY
TRANSLATOR
INPUT

!
Why you . . .
ACME ROCKET
CRASH!!!
I can't look . . .

BONK!
Take that!

WHAM!

STOP!
MY PODS!

Oops.

These are FRIEND PODS, not BATTLE PODS!!!

We're sorry, Bobo.

Input accepted.

Cooling down . . .
TEMP CONTROL

Resetting controls . . .
SYSTEM RESET

Clearing memory cache . . .

ARGLE-BARGLE-GROWLLLLLLLLLLL!!!!!

What's that?!!

RAWR RAWR!
Uh oh.
We must have woken someone up from a nap!

RAWRRAWR! RAWRAWR!!!

Bobo, help!!!

Activate translator.

What translator?! Where?!

HELP!!!!!

BARGLE-ARGLE-BARGLE-FARGLE-BARGLE!!
NO-O-METER
NOPE
CLEAR
METER
MY WAY OR THE HIGHWAY
EMPATHIZER
TRANSLATOR
INPUT

?

BARGLE-ARGLE-BARGLE-FARGLE-BARGLE!!
-O-METER
MY WAY OR THE HIGHWAY
WE COME IN PEACE DONT HURT MY FRIEND

MARGLE-NARGLE-BARGLE-LUMP.

She says:
"When I am woken up from a nap, I feel VERY HANGRY."

She wants us to get OUTER her space!

SNARGLE-BUMP!

Translation:
GLADLY!

Pheweeee!!! I thought I was going to be POD CORN!
What does she want to eat?
CAN WE GET YOU A SNACK?
She says her favorite food is . . . PIGS IN A BLANKET?!
Translation: tiny hot dogs wrapped in puff pastry.
Coming right up.

NOM
NOM NOM
NOM

BURP!
Nap time again?

I can respect that! Let's get OUTER her space!

Roger that, good buddy.

FIRE UP THE TURBO PUMPS!
We can do hard things!

NUT CLUSTER
UPSIDE DOWN
THIS WAY UP
METEOR SHOWER
TOXIC SLUDGE

MEATY-
EROID
PHOBIAS
BLUNDER CLOUD
MEANUS
CUTO
BATTLE
STAR
WORMHOLE
DWARF
PLANET

FOR PETREA, ROMY, AND CAM

—S.M. & E.M.

SPECIAL THANKS TO IMOGEN JAMES FOR HER EPIC PIXEL ART CHARACTER DESIGNS AND ENDLESS INSPIRATION!

Library of Congress Control Number 2023933029

ISBN 978-1-4197-6643-5

Book design by Heather Kelly

Printed and bound in China
10 9 8 7 6 5 4 3 2 1

ABRAMS The Art of Books
195 Broadway, New York, NY 10007
abramsbooks.com